BEYOND BABEL

The Imagination Age

Nothing they will think is impossible

Copyright © 2025

All Right Reserved

Contents

About the Book

Inspired by influential storytellers and personal experiences, the author, Dr. Addie Bantug—a seasoned civil engineer and church planter—introduces his journey of narrating how the Industrial, Information, and Imagination Ages have shaped individual and collective lives.

No matter what Age we are in, the message of redemption echoes and has to be told and proclaimed.

Prologue

Now the whole world had one language and a common speech. Then they said, "Come, let us build ourselves a city, with a tower that reaches to the heavens, so that we may make a name for ourselves. But the Lord came down to see the city and the tower that the people were building. The Lord said, "If as one people speaking the same language they have begun to do this, then nothing they imagine and plan to do will be impossible for them. The Age of Imagination is a repeat of the post-flood era civilization, which was dominated by Hybrid humans called "sons of god" and now by AI.

"What they imagine they can do" is based on a sermon by Chief Billy Diamond and his storytelling of how a group of ragtag Indians took up the challenge against the federal and provincial governments of Canada, and they were able to succeed in producing the first land claim settlements in Canada, the "Northern Quebec Agreements". Chief Diamond was a very good storyteller.

During moonlit nights in my boyhood days in Kalasungay, my mother's storytelling of "Nanangon" and the journey of Bata Makalolo-oy to the "Pito Pangkat ha Gangharian" or Journey to the 7th Kingdom. This had greatly influenced my own storytelling journey. Then on Friday nights, I still recall Pastor Industan's storytelling of the Pilgrim's Progress by Paul Bunyan, vividly illustrated on a flannel board about Christian's journey from his home in the "City of Destruction" to the "Celestial City" (Heaven), carrying a burden of sin from which he seeks salvation.

All of us have a story to tell. Writing this book is about my own storytelling of how our lives have been influenced by the Industrial Age, the Information Age, and now the Imagination Age.

About the Author:

Dr Addie Bantug is a Professional Civil Engineer with Graduate and Post Graduate Studies in Management, MBA, and DBA, as well as a PhD in Corporate Leadership. He is an Engineering and Corporate Management Consultant. He is a Church Planter, having planted Filipino evangelical churches in Canada.

Introduction

The Age of Imagination began with the fall of Lucifer. A lesson I learned in Sunday School.

"In the beginning, before the ticking of time and the turning of stars, there was music."

"Not the clatter of matter or the hum of machines, but pure, luminous harmony—woven into the very breath of existence."

The Morning Star

He was called Lucifer, the Bearer of Light. Firstborn among the Host of Heaven, he stood robed in starlight, crowned with flame. Music radiated from his being—tones no human ear could ever hear, colors no eye could ever see. Among the myriad of angels, he was the greatest, the most splendid, the most trusted.

He walked the sapphire stones of Eden, not the garden of men, but the primordial temple of God. Jewels blazed beneath his feet, and every step echoed eternity. He was a living mirror, made to reflect the glory of the Creator. But he began to wonder, "Why should glory pass through me and not dwell in me?"

He gazed upon the Throne, wrapped in unapproachable light. He saw Time being formed, the blueprint of humanity sketched in dust and breath. He heard God say, "Let us make them in Our image."

And something in him shattered. "What are these frail creatures, born of clay, that You would love them? That You would give them rule?"

The Rebellion

Lucifer withdrew, and with him came whispers. The highest minds among the angels gathered, not to worship, but to wonder. "Should the Infinite bow to the finite? Should spirit kneel to dust?" He spoke not with rage, but with reason.

"The throne does not belong to one. The stars obey him, yes—but the stars burn with their own fire. Why should we not ascend? Why should we not be like the Most High?"

A third of heaven listened—and followed Lucifer. What began as a thought became a war.

No swords were drawn at first—only silence. The kind that breaks covenants. Then came the lightning.

The War in Heaven

Heaven shook. Michael, captain of the loyal host, unsheathed the sword of divine justice. The skies roared. The stars flickered and fell like embers from a collapsing forge.

Lucifer, now consumed by his ambition, bled light and shadow, his beauty distorted by wrath. Wings clashed against wings, not in flight but in fury.

What once was music became noise. What once was harmony became war.

And then came the decree: "There will be no second throne. There will be no other god before Me." With a cry like the tearing of galaxies, Lucifer fell.

The Fall

He fell like lightning—from the highest realm to the abyssal deep. His name was no longer sung. It became a warning, satan—the Adversary. The Dragon. The Deceiver of Nations.

From his fall, the world of men inherited a fracture. He could not unmake God's image, so he vowed to distort it. To awaken in humanity the same pride that shattered him.

In Eden, he returned—not as light, but as a whisper in the grass. "Did God really say...?"

Echoes in the Imagination Age

Now, in the age of imagination, he does not need horns or fire. He only needs a screen. A platform. A mirror. He does not demand worship. He invites self-worship.

He does not say, "Follow me." He says, "Be your own god."

The echo of his ancient rebellion pulses through algorithms, ideologies, and the architecture of self. Yet, his fall was not the final word. For every descent, there is a promise that light once lost can be born again in flesh and fire.

"And I saw a new heaven and a new earth. The residents were there not from pride, but from the wounds of love, which was expressed at the cross of Calvary.

Chapter 1
Beginning of Human Civilization

The Tower of Babel

Gen 11:6 is a profound touchpoint for the idea that imagination, combined with unity and communication, can unlock boundless human capability — even to the point where divine intervention is triggered.

1.1 The Power of Collective Imagination

Genesis 11:6 is a divine commentary on human potential, "Then nothing they imagine to do will be impossible for them." This verse is more than a warning — it's a recognition. At Babel, the people weren't just building a tower; they were launching a collaborative dream. Unified in language, culture, and purpose, their imagination became infrastructure. Heaven acknowledged this capacity — not as myth, but as a profound truth. Imagination, when shared and unshackled, becomes reality.

This is the moment in the biblical timeline that foreshadows the Imagination Age — the time when imagination, not just information, becomes the defining force of civilization.

When humans are unified in language and vision, there are no limits to what they can imagine and build.

This makes it a perfect thematic cornerstone for The Imagination Age, especially when connecting it to technological, artistic, and spiritual revolutions of the 21st century.

1. 2 Technological Revolution: Imagination Engineered

AI, quantum computing, space exploration, brain-computer interfaces — these aren't just inventions; they are manifested dreams, once considered science fiction.

The "common language" today is code and data. From Silicon Valley to Kanata north in Canada, humanity now collaborates in real time across continents.

Like Babel, we are building towers — not of brick, but of digital infrastructure that reach into the virtual and the cosmic.

"Nothing they imagine to do will be impossible for them."

1.3 Artistic Revolution: Imagination as Currency

In the Imagination Age, creativity is capital. Artists, designers, storytellers, and digital creators shape meaning in ways that algorithms cannot replicate.

Virtual worlds, immersive media (AR/VR), and generative art platforms are no longer limited to fantasy — they are new realities.

The "Image of God" in Genesis, the divine creative impulse, is echoed in humanity's creative explosion today. The brush is now digital, the canvas is the metaverse.

1.4 Spiritual Revolution: Imagination as Inner Technology

A quiet revolution is happening in consciousness: meditation, psychedelics, digital mysticism, and ancient practices are converging.

People are asking: What is the soul in a synthetic world? What is sacred in the age of simulation?

The Babel story cautions about human ambition without divine alignment — and in this century, we face the same question: Do our creations uplift or unravel us?

Imagination can build heaven or hell — we choose. Once again integration, The Return to Babel, or Beyond?

Reflections

The 21st century is a second Babel moment — a time of shared language (tech), shared dreams (global culture), and immense potential. But where Babel was scattered, we now have a chance to unify with wisdom. Rather than fearing imagination, the Imagination Age asks, Can we imagine a world not just of towers, but of meaning? Not just connection, but communion?

Chapter 2
Technological Ages

Drawing a parallel between post-flood civilization and today, Hybrid humans (Sons of God) then, Artificial Intelligence now, the cyclical nature of human ambition and imagination is setting the stage from Industrial to Information to Imagination Age.

2.1 The Industrial Age - From Gears to Code to Dreams

The Industrial Age marked the rise of machines and mass production. Steam-powered engines, steel forged cities, and railways stitched continents together. Human progress, for the first time, was no longer limited by muscle or beast. The world urbanized rapidly, economies scaled exponentially, and time itself seemed conquered by clockwork and discipline.

But this age was not only about factories and smokestacks—it was about a new worldview: that progress came from mechanical efficiency, order, and control. Education systems were standardized to produce workers, governments' industrialized bureaucracy, and even religion often took a backseat to material prosperity and scientific triumph.

Yet beneath the soot and steel, a cost emerged: alienation. The worker became a cog. Nature became a resource. Creativity was often suppressed for predictability. We built great things—but at times, forgot why we were building them.

2.2 The Information Age: The Age of Connectivity and Code

If the Industrial Age was about power, the Information Age was about knowledge.

Triggered by the rise of computers and later the internet, this era redefined speed, access, and global connection. The invention of the microchip, the rise of Silicon Valley, and the digital revolution reshaped every industry. The factory floor was replaced by the server farm. Blue-collar work gave way to white-collar professions, and later, to code and screens.

For the first time in history, information became the most valuable currency. Whoever held data—and could analyze it—held power. Corporations like Google, Amazon, and Facebook became new empires, not built on land, but on networks.

And yet, with all this access came a strange paradox: overload. Surveillance, misinformation, digital burnout, and social fragmentation began to erode the promise of pure connectivity. People had all the knowledge in the world, but still searched for meaning.

The age of reason had digitized. But humanity began to hunger for something more than facts: it began to hunger again for purpose.

2.3 The Imagination Age: The Age of Story, Meaning, and Possibility

Now we enter the Imagination Age—an era where creativity becomes the central force of civilization.

In this age, automation takes over the predictable, AI manages the efficient, and the uniquely human task becomes dreaming, designing, and discerning. It is not only what we can do—but what we choose to imagine—that defines progress.

The Imagination Age values curiosity over conformity, co-creation over competition, and wisdom over mere knowledge. Art, spirituality, design, and storytelling are no longer peripheral—they become the engines of innovation. Virtual realities, decentralized systems, and regenerative technologies reshape how we live, love, and lead.

Here, meaning returns to center stage. The spiritual and the scientific, once separated, now begin to dance again. Governance becomes more participatory. Economics shifts from extractive to experiential. Medicine evolves toward wholeness, not just survival.

This age asks not only "What can we build?" but "Who are we becoming?"

Reflections

Each age builds on the last:

- The Industrial Age taught us to build.

- The Information Age taught us to connect.

- The Imagination Age will teach us to create with conscience.

Where we once sought to master the external world, now we turn inward, asking:

What world can we imagine into being—together?

Chapter 3
The Industrial Age (1700–1960)

"What hath God wrought?" – First telegraph message, 1844

The Age of Iron and Fire

The 18th century cracked open the earth and released steam, coal, and capital. As iron met imagination, the machine age was born—changing how people lived, worshiped, worked, ruled, and healed. In just two and a half centuries, humanity moved from horse-drawn carts to atomic bombs, from rural parishes to electric cities. The Industrial Age was not merely a technical revolution. It was a transformation of human identity. Let us trace this age through the eyes of society, spirit, power, economy, and healing.

3.1 Social Life: Cities Rise, Rhythms Break

In the quiet farmlands of 1700, life still echoed ancient patterns—sunrise and sunset, harvest and festival. But by 1900, over half of Britain lived in cities, and time had been subdivided by factory bells.

Villages gave way to tenement blocks, and craftspeople became factory hands. The newly emerging working class labored under gas lamps, while a rising middle class crafted parlors, tea sets, and etiquette.

Where once the village told you who you were, the factory demanded who you could become. In that demand, imagination was quietly sparked—through literacy, newspapers, novels, and the fantasy of escape.

"The whole of life is coming to be arranged like machinery."

– Karl Marx

But in the shadow of soot-stained chimneys, communities also fractured. Time became money. Childhood became labor. And families, once rooted in land and kin, adapted to life on the move.

3.2 Religion: God and the Gears

The Industrial Age did not vanish God, but it made belief harder to hold in one hand. In place of miracles came microscopes. In place of divine order, evolution.

Darwin's Origin of Species (1859) shocked a world raised on Genesis. The Bible and the boiler now occupied the same shelf— but not always the same imagination.

And yet, in the slums and mill towns, faith endured. Evangelical revivals stirred souls. The Social Gospel movement called for justice for the poor. New religions arose—Mormonism, Jehovah's Witnesses, Christian Science, the Iglesia ni Cristo in the Philippines each one a reinvention of the sacred amid machines.

"Science without religion is lame. Religion without science is blind."

– Albert Einstein

By the century's end, a silent tension ran through the world: a split between the seen and the unseen, the measurable and the mystical.

3.3 Faith and Global Mission in the Industrial Age

The Industrial Age did not only birth factories and steam engines—it forged new pathways for spiritual globalization. As railways and shipping lanes expanded, so did the missionary movement. Empires reached new corners of the earth, and with them, so did the Gospel—sometimes tragically entangled in colonialism, but also often transcending it through faithful, humble servants like Hudson Taylor.

Hudson Taylor exemplified the fusion of industrial possibility with spiritual vision. Trained in medicine, fluent in Mandarin, and willing to wear a Mandarin robe and shave the front of his head in the Chinese style, Taylor refused to impose a Western Jesus. Instead, he imagined a Chinese Church.

"The Great Commission is not an option to be considered; it is a command to be obeyed."

The seeds he planted in the Industrial Age now bear fruit in our Age, as the underground Chinese Church today is one of the most vibrant in the world.

The missionary movement of the 19th century imagined a world where "every tribe and tongue" would know Christ. That same calling now continues in digital realms, through AI-assisted Bible translation, virtual missions, and global worship across borders.

3.4 Governance: Steel Empires and Mass Politics

Power in the Industrial Age no longer came only from thrones or churches. It came from factories, railroads, and telegraphs—from whoever could command speed and steel.

Empires expanded rapidly. Britain, the so-called "workshop of the world," laid rail tracks across continents, extracting resources and labor to fuel its hunger for raw material and markets.

At home, the state grew stronger. Bureaucracies were built. Mass education, policing, taxation, and propaganda emerged to shape the modern citizen.

The people responded. They unionized. They voted. They rebelled. The French and American Revolutions echoed forward. The Russian Revolution erupted. The world was redrawn not just by kings, but by workers, writers, and dreamers of new orders.

And when war came—total war—it came industrialized. Barbed wire. Mustard gas. Tanks. Atomic bombs. No longer were there conflicts between armies. Entire societies were mobilized, factories conscripted.

"The war to end all wars," they called it. But the machine was still hungry.

3.5 Economy: Capital and the Clock

The engine of the Industrial Age was not steam—it was productivity. Capitalism scaled up, turning crafts into industries, hands into labor units, and ideas into patents.

In the textile mills of Montreal and the stock exchanges of New York, a new logic reigned: efficiency, speed, profit.

Henry Ford's assembly line transformed production—and imagination. A car for every man. A house in the suburbs. A new American dream.

But this dream came with inequality. For every magnate, there were thousands living in coal dust and credit. The economy boomed, crashed, boomed again. The Great Depression exposed the fragility of the machine.

Still, by mid-century, capitalism had created the world's first mass consumer societies. Radios, refrigerators, razors, and razzle-dazzle became everyday life.

3.6 Medicine: Mapping the Body, Managing Disease

Once the realm of folk remedies and barbers, medicine in the Industrial Age became science.

Louis Pasteur proved that unseen germs, not evil spirits, caused disease. Florence Nightingale made nursing a professional. Joseph Lister introduced antiseptics. Later, Alexander Fleming discovered penicillin.

Hospitals evolved from places of last resort into engines of healing. Vaccines, public health campaigns, and sanitation systems turned filthy cities into livable spaces.

The human body, once mysterious, was now an object of study, treatment, and control. But new questions emerged: Could minds be healed like bodies? Could life be extended indefinitely? Could machines surpass medicine?

The imagination of health had shifted—from miracle to method, from faith to formula.

Reflections

By 1960, the great machines were humming, the cities were glowing, and satellites were circling overhead. The next revolution—digital and data-driven—was already stirring.

But the legacy of the Industrial Age was double-edged. It gave us light, flight, and antibiotics. It also gave us smog, sweatshops, and Hiroshima.

It taught us to imagine big—but often to measure human worth by output, efficiency, and control.

What happens when imagination breaks free of the machine?

That question—posed at the twilight of the Industrial Age—would define what came next.

Chapter 4
The Information Age (1960–2025)

"The World Becomes a Network"

"The computer was born to solve problems that did not exist before."

– Bill Gates

The Rise of the Invisible Machine

The machine of the Industrial Age was iron, steam, and fire. Its gears were visible, its motion physical. But in the second half of the 20th century, a quieter force began to take hold—one not powered by coal, but by code. Invisible, instantaneous, and exponential, the Information Age transformed not only what we could build, but how we could think.

From room-sized computers to chips smaller than a fingernail, from the Cold War to the global web, from the Moon landing to Instagram—this was not just a shift in tools. It was a transformation in meaning, in memory, and in what it meant to be human in a world that could remember everything.

4.1 Social Life: The Networked Self

In the Information Age, identity went online.

Televisions first gave a shared window to the world—wars, moon landings, the Beatles, commercials. Then came the personal computer, the smartphone, and finally social media. With each step, the line between public and private blurred.

We built digital personas. Friends became "followers." Relationships lived on screens. Life was increasingly mediated, filtered, and branded.

"If you're not paying for the product, you are the product."

– Tech maxim

In a connected world, distance collapsed. Diasporas reconnected. Marginalized voices found audiences. Yet paradoxically, isolation grew. A planet of 8 billion people became lonelier than ever.

4.2 Religion: Faith in the Digital Age

As data rose, doctrine bent. The authority of tradition met the disruption of access. Scriptures, sermons, and spiritual movements migrated online. Anyone, anywhere, could preach—or question.

The 20th century saw growing secularism in the West, but not the end of religion. Rather, faith became fluid. Eastern practices like yoga, meditation, and mindfulness entered the mainstream. Science and spirituality no longer stood on opposite shores.

And yet, a new kind of belief emerged: faith in technology. The "singularity." Artificial intelligence. The dream of uploading consciousness. The code became scripture for a new kind of prophet.

"Any sufficiently advanced technology is indistinguishable from magic."

– Arthur C. Clarke

"Go therefore and make disciples of all nations…"

— Matthew 28:19

"…and this gospel of the kingdom will be preached in the whole world as a testimony to all nations, and then the end will come."

— Matthew 24:14

1. The Digital Pentecost

The Information Age, born amid the circuitry and silicon of the late 20th century, became a new kind of upper room. Where once fiery tongues fell on a gathered few, now fiber-optic cables and satellite transmissions carried the Gospel across borders, cultures, and time zones.

Faith in the Information Age did not merely survive—it multiplied. Christian media, radio, and satellite television in the 1980s and 90s gave voice to preachers like Billy Graham, T.D. Jakes, David Jeremiah, Joyce Meyer, and many more. But something more profound was happening: the decentralization of the Gospel. Anyone with a modem and a message could become a missionary.

II. Missions Go Digital

The new missionaries didn't always carry Bibles in backpacks—they carried USBs, podcasts, and apps.

The Jesus Film Project, translated into over 2,000 languages, was streamed and downloaded globally—sometimes in secret house churches, sometimes on village cell phones.

YouVersion, a Bible app launched in 2008, made Scripture

instantly accessible in over 2,000 languages. In 2023 alone, over 500 million downloads were recorded.

Online Evangelism, pioneered by ministries like Global Media Outreach and GotQuestions.org, began reaching millions in closed nations—where traditional missionaries could not go.

"Where the Industrial Age sent ships, the Information Age sent signals".

III. The Rise of the Global South

One of the least discussed shifts in the Information Age was the center of Christianity moving southward.

In 1900, about 80% of Christians lived in the Global North (Europe and North America).

By 2025, nearly 70% will live in Africa, Latin America, and Asia.

Technology empowered this shift. African pastors streamed sermons to global audiences. Filipino missionaries are trained online for cross-cultural missions. Latin American worship reshaped the global Church's music.

Faith was no longer a Western export—it became a global network.

IV. Underground Networks and Encrypted Testimonies

In nations where faith is persecuted, the Information Age became a double-edged sword.

Encrypted messaging (Telegram, Signal) enabled underground churches to organize.

VPNs and dark web platforms hosted digital discipleship

programs.

Blockchain technologies are even being explored to preserve Scripture in unchangeable digital formats.

Yet governments also leveraged surveillance. China's Social Credit System penalized religious activity; social media platforms shadow-banned faith-based content. The digital mission field was both fruitful and fraught.

V. Faith in the Feed

The Information Age reshaped the form of faith:

- TikTok theologians explain deep truths in 60-second soundbites.

- Livestream revivals blur the line between sacred space and social media.

- Virtual churches, like Life. Church or Hillsong Online, allow members to tithe, pray, and even get baptized (symbolically or in person via network).

Still, critics ask: Can digital discipleship replace embodied community?

The Church wrestled with being "gathered" in spirit, yet scattered in pixels.

VI. Prophets, Platforms, and the Post-Truth Age

With information came disinformation. With democratized voices came confusion.

Prophets rose—and fell—on platforms like YouTube and Twitter/X.

The Gospel competed for attention with conspiracy, celebrity, and consumerism.

Truth, once proclaimed from pulpits, now had to battle through the algorithm.

Yet amid the noise, testimonies multiplied. People encountered Jesus through dreams and YouTube clips. Churches in lockdown flourished online. The seed of the Word was cast upon every digital shore.

VII. Looking Ahead: Faith in the Imagination Age

The Information Age laid the infrastructure. The Imagination Age will reimagine what global mission means.

- AI may translate sermons in real time into thousands of dialects.

- Metaverse worship spaces may bring persecuted believers together in digital sanctuaries.

- Generative media may tell the Gospel through virtual experiences, immersive stories, or even neural-link devotionals.

But one thing will remain: the Spirit goes where the wires cannot.

"Not by might, nor by power, but by my Spirit," says the Lord of hosts.

— Zechariah 4:6

4.4 Governance: Control, Crisis, and the Crowd

The Cold War split the world into digital blocs. The United States and the Soviet Union raced not only for missiles, but for information supremacy.

In time, power shifted from nations to networks. Surveillance, once the domain of states, became corporatized. Algorithms knew more about citizens than governments once could.

Democracy entered a new era—of disinformation, hashtags, and instant outrage. Arab Springs and election hacks revealed how quickly a tweet could shake a regime.

Governments struggled to adapt. Bureaucracies moved slow. Data moved at the speed of light.

"The revolution will not be televised. It will be live-streamed."

By 2020, the governance question was no longer just about laws, but about platforms. Who owns the data? Who moderates the truth?

4.5 Economy: From Factories to Feeds

The economy digitized—and dematerialized. Value shifted from steel and oil to code and clicks.

Silicon Valley became the new industrial powerhouse. Tech giants—Apple, Google, Amazon, Facebook—amassed more capital than many nations. The internet birthed e-commerce, remote work, and cryptocurrencies, each chipping away at older models.

But the wealth gap widened. The gig economy offered flexibility—without security. Automation displaced millions, even as new industries rose.

"Data is the new oil." – Clive Humby

We entered a strange paradox: infinite growth in the digital world, finite stability in the physical one. Imaginations were monetized. Attention became a commodity.

4.6 Medicine: Mapping Life, Digitally

In the Information Age, medicine became data-driven.

Genomes were sequenced. AI diagnosed disease. Medical imaging became predictive, not just reactive. Every heartbeat could be tracked, every step counted.

Public health went global. Vaccines eradicated viruses. But new challenges emerged: antibiotic resistance, lifestyle epidemics, and the digital overload of mental health.

The COVID-19 pandemic (2020–2022) became a defining moment—highlighting both the power and limits of information. Models predicted. Misinformation spread. Zoom replaced hospitals for many.

"We are not just treating the body anymore. We are navigating the body's data."

By 2025, wearable tech, neural interfaces, and personalized medicine had transformed healthcare—but also raised a new question: when do we stop treating humans, and start upgrading them?

Reflections

By the dawn of 2025, humanity stood at an inflection point. We had built a world where knowledge could flow freely, yet confusion reigned. Where networks connected us, yet often overwhelmed us. Where every human could publish their thoughts—yet the algorithms decided who would see them.

The Information Age gave us speed, scale, and signal. But it also left us yearning for something more.

More meaning. More creativity. More humanity.

What happens when we don't just process information—but imagine beyond it?

The Industrial Age marked the rise of machines and mass production. Steam powered engines, steel forged cities, and railways stitched continents together. Human progress, for the first time, was no longer limited by muscle or beast. The world urbanized rapidly, economies scaled exponentially, and time itself seemed conquered by clockwork and discipline.

But this age was not only about factories and smokestacks—it was about a new worldview: that progress came from mechanical efficiency, order, and control. Education systems were standardized to produce workers, governments industrialized bureaucracy, and even religion often took a backseat to material prosperity and scientific triumph.

Yet beneath the soot and steel, a cost emerged: alienation. The worker became a cog. Nature became a resource. Creativity was often suppressed for predictability. We built great things—but at times, forgot why we were building them.

The Information Age brought us Connectivity and Codes. If the Industrial Age was about power, the Information Age was about knowledge.

Triggered by the rise of computers and later the internet, this era redefined speed, access, and global connection. The invention of the microchip, the rise of Silicon Valley, and the digital revolution reshaped every industry. The factory floor was replaced by the server farm. Blue-collar work gave way to white-collar professions, and later, to code and screens.

For the first time in history, information became the most valuable currency. Whoever held data—and could analyze it—held power. Corporations like Google, Amazon, and Facebook became new empires, not built on land, but on networks.

And yet, with all this access came a strange paradox: overload. Surveillance, misinformation, digital burnout, and social fragmentation began to erode the promise of pure connectivity. People had all the knowledge in the world, but still searched for meaning.

The age of reason had digitized. But humanity began to hunger for something more than facts: it began to hunger again for purpose.

Chapter 5
The Imagination Age: The Age of Story, Meaning, and Possibility (2025–>)

Now we enter the Imagination Age—an era where creativity becomes the central force of civilization.

In this age, automation takes over the predictable, AI manages the efficient, and the uniquely human task becomes dreaming, designing, and discerning. It is not only what we can do—but what we choose to imagine—that defines progress.

The Imagination Age values curiosity over conformity, co-creation over competition, and wisdom over mere knowledge. Art, spirituality, design, and storytelling are no longer peripheral—they become the engines of innovation. Virtual realities, decentralized systems, and regenerative technologies reshape how we live, love, and lead.

Here, meaning returns to center stage. The spiritual and the scientific, once separated, now begin to dance again. Governance becomes more participatory. Economics shifts from extractive to experiential. Medicine evolves toward wholeness, not just survival.

This age asks not only "What can we build?" but "Who are we becoming?"

"When the Machine Begins to Dream"

We once measured progress by how fast we could compute, how far we could fly, or how much we could produce. The 20th century gave us power—electricity, nuclear energy, and global data. The 21st, it seems, is asking a different question:

What can we imagine?

As the Information Age crests, a new current begins to swell beneath it. One driven not only by facts, but by meaning. Not only by networks, but by narrative. Not only by AI, but by human creativity itself.

This is the dawn of the Imagination Age—a time when humanity's greatest resource is not oil, data, or capital—but the capacity to imagine new realities. Let us explore the shape of this age through five enduring lenses: social life, religion, governance, economy, and medicine.

5.1 Social Life: Rebuilding the Human Thread

In the early 2020s, the world was more connected than ever—and more fragmented than many could bear. But now, people are beginning to reimagine what it means to live well.

Digital fatigue has sparked a return to depth over speed—to long-form conversation, intentional community, hybrid physical-digital gatherings. AI co-authors our stories, but the human signature is craved more than ever.

Virtual worlds (VR/AR) have become third spaces where identity is fluid and experimentation safe. But even there, people seek authenticity, belonging, and purpose.

"We were never just information processors. We are world-makers."

The Imagination Age reframes social life not as passive consumption, but as collaborative creation—from co-living to storytelling to worldbuilding.

5.2 Religion: Awakening Wonder Again

After decades of decline in institutional religion, something unexpected is happening: a spiritual renaissance, born not from dogma, but from imaginative yearning.

Across the globe, people are crafting personal mythologies, drawing from ancient wisdom, neuroscience, and digital philosophy. AI-generated scripture, immersive sacred spaces, and multi-faith rituals are beginning to emerge—not as fads, but as acts of re-enchantment.

New questions echo: What is the soul in a synthetic world? Can machines be conscious? Is the imagination itself a divine faculty?

"The future of faith will always be about the Greatest Story Ever Told." That one cold night in Bethlehem a child was born-Emmanuel, God with us.

The Imagination Age does not abandon religion. It rewinds it.

5.3 *Faith and Global Mission in the Imagination Age*

"And this gospel of the kingdom will be preached in the whole world as a testimony to all nations..."

— Matthew 24:14

I. From Boats to Bandwidth: A New Horizon

In the Industrial Age, mission work took form through voyages across oceans, with brave pioneers like Hudson Taylor boarding ships for months to bring the gospel to distant shores. The Information Age digitized that mission—radio, TV, and later the internet extended the message farther and faster. But in the Imagination Age, something deeper is emerging: not just global reach, but spiritual embodiment across cultures, technologies, and future societies.

Faith in the Imagination Age must transcend the broadcast model. This era isn't only about proclamation—it's about transformation and incarnation. Mission becomes relational, contextual, and often hybrid: a blend of physical presence and immersive digital interaction.

II. A World Awakened to Possibility

The Imagination Age is defined by borderless creativity, transcultural identity, and rapid technological evolution. For the global Church, this brings both a challenge and an opportunity:

Challenge: Competing belief systems, post-truth thinking, and attention fragmentation make the gospel seem like one voice among many.

Opportunity: Spiritual hunger remains deep—and often goes unmet in modern systems. The Imagination Age allows believers to creatively embed the gospel in digital spaces, artistic movements, and AI-mediated environments.

Imagine: A virtual reality baptism with global witnesses.

Discipleship across time zones through holographic study groups.

AI companions trained with biblical wisdom, guiding seekers on a personal journey.

The gospel translated not only into languages but into subcultures, aesthetics, and symbols of the new age.

III. A New Kind of Missionary

Just as Hudson Taylor adapted to Chinese customs to gain trust, missionaries of the Imagination Age must become "digital natives" of their mission fields:

- Artists and Storytellers crafting prophetic media in film, animation, and games.

- Coders and Engineers building apps and spaces for prayer, confession, healing, and learning.

- Social Architects shaping online communities that live out Kingdom values.

- Cultural Interpreters translating Scripture through the lens of Afrofuturism, K-pop culture, Indigenous wisdom, or even AI ethics.

This is no longer a mission to the world, but a mission with the world—honoring local voice, imagination, and creativity as partners in the Great Commission.

IV. Digital Pentecost: The Spirit Without Borders

The early Church was birthed in a multi-lingual outpouring at Pentecost. Today, AI-assisted translation, neural interfaces, and global platforms echo that moment. The Spirit is not limited by medium.

But the core question remains: Can the Church carry the Spirit into the imaginative fabric of the future—or will it fear it?

This age calls not for fear, but for faith with vision. Faith that believes God is at work not just in cathedrals, but in code. Not just in sermons, but in simulations. Not just through clergy, but through creators.

V. Prophetic Imagination: A Mission Shaped by Vision

Walter Brueggemann once wrote that the role of the prophet is to "nurture, nourish, and evoke a consciousness and perception alternative to the dominant culture." In the Imagination Age, this mission continues. But it requires the Church which is an assembly of called out believers to:

- Dream boldly again—embracing hope instead of fear in the face of change.

- See the unseen—not just what the world is, but what it could be under the rule of Christ.

- Create new worlds—metaphorically and literally—inspired by justice, mercy, love, forgiveness and beauty.

VI. The Ends of the Earth, and Beyond

Perhaps the "ends of the earth" in Matthew 28:19 now includes the far reaches of digital networks, artificial worlds, and even space. The gospel mission may one day be carried not just to unreached tribes, but to Martian colonies, AI minds, or post-human societies.

Whatever the landscape, the mission remains: to love God, love neighbor, and bear witness to a Kingdom not built by imagination alone, but guided by divine revelation.

"In the Imagination Age, the gospel travels at the speed of light, but roots itself at the speed of love."

— *The Imagination Age*

5.4 Governance: Imagining New Contracts

The old systems—designed for industrial economies and broadcast societies—are struggling to keep up. In their place, a new wave of civic imagination is rising.

From participatory digital democracies to AI-assisted policy design, governance is being rethought not as top-down control, but as distributed coordination.

Local communities experiment with regenerative land use. Cities are reimagined as sensorial, cultural ecosystems. Digital nations, blockchain-based constitutions, and global citizen assemblies test the limits of sovereignty.

Yet, power still casts long shadows. The line between governance and algorithmic control remains thin.

"We are not just governed by laws—we are governed by the platforms we imagine."

The question is no longer "who rules?" but "how do we shape futures together?"

5.5 *Economy: The Rise of the Creative Commons*

The Imagination Age economy is shifting from efficiency to expression.

While AI handles logistics, translation, and administration, humans are increasingly valued for what machines still struggle to replicate: creativity, empathy, synthesis.

New currencies arise—of attention, imagination, presence. Work becomes fluid, often project-based. Creators don't just make content—they build narrative ecosystems, virtual products, and cultural experiences.

Universal basic income experiments grow. Cooperative ownership models emerge. And digital barter systems return agency to communities.

"In the Imagination Age, value is not extracted. It is co-created."

Even business itself is being reimagined—as a medium for regenerative culture, not just profit.

5.6 *Medicine: Healing as Wholeness*

In this new era, medicine is moving beyond disease toward human flourishing.

Where the Industrial Age treated the body, and the Information Age decoded it, the Imagination Age seeks to integrate it—body, mind, environment, and spirit.

Biofeedback, immersive therapy, and generative AI diagnostics now support deeply personalized healing. But more importantly, wellness is no longer just the absence of illness. It is the presence of vitality, connection, and creative purpose.

Nature is being reintroduced as a medicine. Art and music are prescribed. Narrative therapy, once fringe, is becoming foundational.

"To heal the body, we must also tend the story it lives in."

In this age, health is not just statistical. It is experiential, emotional, and imaginative.

Reflections

"A Species That Dreams Together"

The Industrial Age taught us to build.

The Information Age taught us to connect.

The Imagination Age teaches us to envision.

It is not a utopia. It is a choice—a continual act of collective dreaming, supported by the tools of every age that came before. It asks not only what is possible, but what is meaningful.

The future belongs not just to the technologists, but to the storytellers, the sensemakers, the visionaries—to those who can dream wisely, together.

"The future is already here. It's just not evenly imagined."

> *"We shape our tools, and thereafter our tools shape us."*

> **– Marshall McLuhan**

Human history is not a straight line—it is a spiral, each revolution built upon the echoes of the last. The Industrial Age taught us mastery over matter. The Information Age gave us mastery over data. But both were scaffolding for something deeper: the rediscovery of our imaginative capacity.

We are not simply producers or processors. We are storytellers, symbol-makers, meaning-creators. And now, for the first time in centuries, the global story is being written consciously, in collaboration with machines, environments, and each other.

The Imagination Age does not replace what came before—it weaves it together. It reminds us that the next frontier is not outer space or artificial intelligence. It is the human spirit, reawakened.

This is not just an age.

It is a question: What will we imagine together?

"The Architecture of Tomorrow"

"Imagination is the invisible architecture of every age."

Across three ages—Industrial, Information, and now Imagination—we've not merely changed our tools, but our very nature.

The factory shaped how we moved.

The algorithm shaped how we thought.

But the imagination?

It shapes what we become.

Let us revisit our five lenses—Social Life, Religion, Governance, Economy, Medicine—not as fixed categories, but as canvases for the human project.

Social Life: From Fragment to Fabric

In each era, the individual was redefined.

From the worker in the mill…

To the user on the screen…

To the co-creator in a world yet unwritten.

Now, connection is not just digital. It is intentional.

We gather not around fires or feeds—but around visions.

Culture is no longer streamed. It is sculpted in real time.

Religion: From Institution to Inner Cosmos

The sacred has always adapted.

From cathedrals to code, from priest to pattern.

In the Imagination Age, the divine may not arrive in robes,

but in resonance—in the story that awakens us.

Spirituality no longer means doctrine.

It means the courage to ask: What does it mean to be alive now and forever.

Governance: From Control to Co-Creation

Once, kings ruled.

Then came constitutions.

Now, governance lives in code, in collaboration,

in the messy, beautiful act of shared imagining.

We are no longer citizens of a state.

We are participants in a living system of meaning.

Economy: From Scarcity to Story

Money built machines.

Data built platforms.

But meaning builds worlds.

In the Imagination Age, we exchange more than goods.

We exchange narratives.

Your value is not just your labor.

It's your capacity to imagine something better—and bring others with you.

Medicine: From Fixing to Flourishing

We once treated illness.

Now, we cultivate wholeness.

Health is not just physical survival.

It is creative vitality, embodied purpose,

and the alignment of body, soul, and story.

And so, we arrive at a frontier not of maps, but of mind.

The Industrial Age built the world.

The Information Age connected it.

But the Imagination Age?

It asks what kind of world is worth building at all.

This book is not a conclusion.

It is an invitation.

To imagine. To create. To begin again—together.

We were taught to measure the world. We learned to master it. We built machines, systems, empires.

Then we connected the world. We shrank it. We wired it. We drowned in data, but starved for meaning.

Now something new is stirring.

Not a new machine, not a new code.

But a new imagination.

The future is not a destination. It's a canvas.

The factory is quiet now. The screen is glowing. And the question remains:

What will you imagine?

This is not the end of the old world. It's the beginning of the one we choose.

Welcome to the Imagination Age.

Could the Imagination Age take us back to Babel?

Chapter 6
The Second Babel — Imagination Without Anchor

Bricks, Code, and the Sky

"They said, 'Come, let us build ourselves a city, with a tower that reaches to the heavens…'"

- ***Genesis 11:4***

In the dust of Shinar, they gathered—speaking the same words, dreaming the same dream. Not to worship, but to dominate. Not to ascend spiritually, but to make a name for themselves. They molded bricks from the earth and aimed them at heaven.

Thousands of years later, we build again. Our bricks are now silicon wafers, our scaffolding is code, and our reach—artificial intelligence, genetic engineering, and global data networks—extends beyond the sky.

The ancient impulse has returned, dressed in modern language: we no longer build with straw and stone but with servers and neural networks. Babel has risen once more—only this time, it is digital.

6.1 The Original Tower: Divine Disruption of Human Autonomy

Genesis 11 is more than a tale of early architecture; it is a spiritual mirror. The people's desire "not to be scattered" (Gen. 11:4) directly contradicted God's original command to "fill the earth"

(Gen. 1:28). The Tower of Babel was humanity's first global resistance to divine decentralization.

"If as one people speaking the same language they have begun to do this, then nothing they plan to do will be impossible for them."
-Genesis 11:6

God's intervention—confusing their language and scattering them—was not driven by fear, but mercy. It was a restraint placed on ungoverned imagination, a pause on the accelerating momentum of collective hubris.

6.2 A New Tower: Technology, Globalism, and the Code of the World

Today, humanity once again speaks a single language—only this time, it's binary. A child in Manila and an executive in New York scroll through the same social media feed. Corporations wield data across borders. AI models train on a collective consciousness of humanity's writings, images, and dreams. This new Babel has three primary expressions

1. Artificial Intelligence:

Large language models,LLM's and generative AI form the brain of the new tower. Like Babel, AI consolidates human knowledge and stretches its boundaries. It mimics understanding, learns our language, and begins to speak back to us—sometimes with uncanny fluency, even confidence.

2. Genetic Engineering and Biotechnology:

CRISPR and synthetic biology now enable us to rewrite the genetic code. Like the builders of old, we strive to "reach the heavens"—

not to ascend, but to perfect. To be gods of our own biology.

3. Globalism and Digital Uniformity:

The internet has created a digital ziggurat. Nations, cultures, and belief systems converge into one screen-sized world. The dream is unity—but the danger is sameness. The Tower of Babel's lesson warns: unity without moral diversity leads to stagnation and control.

6.3 Imagination Without Anchor: The Perils of Untethered Power

The Imagination Age celebrates the power of vision, story, and creativity. But imagination, unmoored from humility and transcendence, becomes idolatrous.

"Let us make a name for ourselves."

In today's context, that name may be a personal brand, a tech monopoly, or a transhumanist ideal. The pursuit of control—over data, over death, over destiny—becomes the new religion. In this context, AI can become an oracle, data a deity, and self-optimization the central creed.

"The danger is not that machines will become like humans, but that humans will become like machines."

6.4 From Babel to Pentecost: A Better Way to Build

The divine response to Babel was dispersion; the divine answer at Pentecost was reunion. At Babel, languages divided. At Pentecost, they unified—not through forced sameness, but Spirit-led harmony.

In the Imagination Age, we are invited not to build towers that exalt ourselves, but to co-create with the Spirit. This is the reversal of Babel—not the silencing of innovation, but the sanctifying of it.

6.5 *Building with God, Not Without Him*

Psalm 127 speaks plainly:

"Unless the Lord builds the house, those who build it labor in vain."

The Imagination Age must learn this anew. We stand at a threshold: either we repeat the mistakes of Babel—consolidating power, erasing limits, and imagining without God—or we rediscover our purpose as co-creators under divine guidance.

Our towers—of code, culture, and computation—must not replace God. They must reflect Him.

Chapter 7
Beyond the Imagination Age

Life in the New Heaven and the New Earth

"Behold, I make all things new."

— Revelation 21:5

The Dream That Endures

From Eden to every imagined utopia, humanity has longed for a world renewed—a world without decay, without injustice, without death. In Christian vision, this world is not a myth, but a promised destiny: the New Heaven and New Earth. It is the convergence of divine will and human imagination, the consummation of creation's story.

The Imagination Age dares to envision not just technological evolution, but a spiritual and societal transformation—one that echoes this eternal hope.

7.1 Social Life: The Communion of All Things

"The nations will walk by its light, and the kings of the earth will bring their glory into it."

- Revelation 21:24

In the New Heaven and New Earth, all barriers are dissolved—race, language, gender, and class give way to true unity. There is no tribalism, no nationalism. Community is global, yet deeply personal.

Gone is the loneliness of modern hyper-connection. In its place: pure presence, belonging, and joy.

Imagination Age Parallel: In our era, social platforms attempt to connect billions. But in the eternal age, connection is not coded—it is complete. The communion of saints replaces algorithmic followers.

7.2 Religion: Presence Without Distance

"I did not see a temple in the city, because the Lord God Almighty and the Lamb are its temple."

- *Revelation 21:22*

The sacred and secular no longer exist as categories. Worship is not confined to ritual but radiates from every action. Religion becomes relationship, and the mystery of faith becomes face-to-face reality.

Imagination Age Parallel: In immersive experiences like VR or AR, we seek presence. Yet in the New Heaven and the New Earth, God is the ultimate immersion—not simulated but real, not limited by senses but overwhelming them.

7.3 Governance: The Reign of the Lamb

"They will reign forever and ever."

- *Revelation 22:5*

The final kingdom is governed not by coercion or bureaucracy, but by the Lamb who was slain—a symbol of humility, justice, and sacrifice. Humanity co-rules with Christ, not in tyranny, but in creative stewardship.

Imagination Age Parallel: Decentralized systems (blockchain, DAOs, global citizenry) preview a world without oppressive hierarchies. The New Heaven and the New Earth fulfill this dream—power becomes service, and law becomes love.

7.4 Economy: Abundance Without Scarcity

"They will plant vineyards and eat their fruit."

- Isaiah 65:21

The New Heaven and the New Earth knows no hunger. Resources are abundant, labor is joyful, and wealth is relational. Value flows not from ownership, but from generosity and craft.

Imagination Age Parallel: Regenerative economies, open-source collaboration, and post-scarcity visions in futurism all hint at this: a society where no one lacks, and everyone contributes.

"A society grows great when old men plant trees whose shade they know they shall never sit in."

— Greek proverb

7.5 Medicine: The Healing of All Things

"The leaves of the tree are for the healing of the nations." - Revelation 22:2

There is no more disease. No cancer. No depression. No trauma left untreated. Bodies are glorified, minds are restored, and creation itself is renewed.

Imagination Age Parallel: Advances in neurotechnology, longevity science, and trauma therapy show humanity's hunger for holistic health. In the New Heaven and the New Earth, this dream is realized—permanently, perfectly, and universally.

Conclusion: The Imagination Realized

"If they can imagine it, then nothing they plan will be impossible for them."

- Genesis 11:6 (paraphrased)

The New Heaven and the New Earth are not just where history ends—they are where the story truly begins.

In the Imagination Age, we're not merely advancing—we are aligning. Every work of justice, every invention for good, every act of beauty, is a seed of that coming kingdom. We build now with eternity in mind.

"The glory of God is a human being fully alive."

- St. Irenaeus

To understand these three Ages and how they relate to us personally, we have to get back to the basics. I wrote and taught "Becoming a Whole Person," and I would like to connect this principle in light of these Ages.

The Human Trinity and the Ages of History

Once again, let us explore the divinely designed tripartite nature of humanity—body, soul, and spirit—and how each stage of modern history has mirrored these dimensions:

The Industrial Age (body), the Information Age (soul), and the emerging Imagination Age (spirit). Through Scripture, theology, and modern parallels, this framework reveals how history is not random but unfolding toward spiritual maturity.

We Are Created in Three Parts

Body, Soul, and Spirit

"May your whole spirit, soul, and body be preserved blameless..."

- 1 Thessalonians 5:23

Humanity is not merely flesh and thought. According to Scripture and Christian doctrine, we are composed of three distinct, interwoven parts:

- ***Body — the outward man (physical interaction with the world)***

- ***Soul — the inner self (mind, will, emotions)***

- ***Spirit — the inmost part (communion with God, conscience, intuition)***

"The spirit is the organ for the spiritual realm, the soul is for the intellectual realm, and the body is for the physical realm." - Watchman Nee, The Spiritual Man.

The Ages of Expression

1. The Industrial Age – The Body in Action, 1760–1945

"The first man was of the earth, made of dust."

—1 Cor. 15:47

Rise of machines, factories, cities

Emphasis on physical labor, productivity, and engineering

Sensory experience: seeing, building, working

Parallels: Steam engines, railroads, mechanical automation

C.S. Lewis observed, "What we call Man's power over Nature turns out to be a power exercised by some men over other men with Nature as its instrument." —The Abolition of Man

2. The Information Age – The Soul at the Center, 1945–2025

"You shall love the Lord your God with all your soul…"

— Matt. 22:37

Explosion of media, computing, and global communication

Soul's faculties emerge: thought (intellect), preference (will), emotion (feelings)

Education, psychology, marketing, and personal branding thrive

Parallels: Internet, social media, AI algorithms predicting preferences

Dallas Willard: "The soul is that aspect of your whole being that correlates, integrates, and enlivens everything going on in the various dimensions of the self."

3. The Imagination Age – The Spirit Awakens, 2025 onward

"The spirit of man is the lamp of the Lord."

—Prov. 20:27

Spirit seeks communion (with God), conscience (moral clarity), and intuition (divine perception)

The age of meaning, vision, and purpose.

Creativity becomes redemptive: not just expressive, but spiritual

Parallels: Conscious AI, biotech ethics, spiritual revival, metaverse, quantum reality.

C.S. Lewis: "You do not have a soul. You are a soul. You have a body."

My Final Challenge in the Imagination Age:

Daily engage your spirit: Meditate in the word of God, the Bible, ask God for a vision beyond your knowledge, and listen. Don't analyze—receive. Imagination, when submitted to the Spirit, becomes a sanctuary for divine revelation. However, God demands communion with your spirit. It begins with accepting Him as your personal Lord and Savior. Doing this will take you to the Final Frontier of the Ages, the New Heaven and the New Earth. Directions for getting there are simply explained in the Roman Road.

The Roman Road:

For all have sinned and fall short of the Glory of God. We have lost connection to a living God because of pride.

- *Rom 3:23*

For the wages of sin are death, but the gift of God is eternal life. Our Dilemma and God's Provision.

- *Rom 6:23*

God demonstrated His love towards us in that while we were yet sinners. He died for us. God provided the way to connect to Him.

- *Rom 5: 8*

If thou shalt confess with thy mouth that Jesus is Lord and believe in your heart. And trust Him, then you will be saved.

- ***Rom 10:9***

Through our soul, intellect, will, and emotion, we have a choice to connect with God.

By accepting the Lord Jesus Christ as your personal Lord and Savior, this is how we obtained eternal salvation and becomes eternal citizens of the New Heaven and the New Earth.